# Katie Mou

# Christmas Door



Words and Pictures by

Anne L. Watson

Skyhook Press
Bellingham, Washington

"Less than two weeks till Christmas!" said Mama Mouse to Papa and Katie and Dylan. "We will have to scamper to get ready."

"Let's hang lights on the house, this year," said Papa Mouse. "Right to the top of the tower."

"How?" asked Mama. "Our ladder won't reach that high."

"It doesn't have to!" said Papa. "I'll hire Reddy Cardinal and his flight crew. They don't need ladders at all!"

"What about our Christmas tree?" said Katie.

"I'll go to the tree farm this weekend," said Papa. "Anyone want to come along?"

"I do!" Katie squeaked.

"Me, too!" said Dylan. "Ride train!"

Papa laughed. "I think we'll need the car, but we might see a train on the way."

Mama said, "While Papa's doing all that, I'll hang the Christmas quilt, and put the Christmas village on the mantel, and make paper stars, and bake cookies for Santa Mouse . . ."

Katie just loved when Mama got ready for Christmas!

MOUSE TOWN

It snowed so much that night, Katie's school closed the next day. About an hour after breakfast, she heard the doorbell.

It was Billy Squirrel. "Can you come out and play?" he asked. "We're building a snowmouse!"

Katie bundled up and ran outside. Almost everyone was out playing. And they were all excited about Christmas.

"Santa Mouse might bring me a bicycle," Billy said.

"I hope I get ice skates," said Charlie Chipmunk.

"What do *you* want, Katie?" Billy asked.

"I don't know," said Katie. "I can't decide."

"You could ask for a bicycle, too," Billy said.

"But I like the one I have," said Katie. "I don't think I need a new one."

A couple of days later, Reddy Cardinal came in his truck. Papa brought out box after box of Christmas lights.

"That's a lot of lights!" Reddy said. "They'll light up the whole neighborhood!"

"I hope so," said Papa, rubbing his paws together for warmth. "I love Christmas lights. String them all the way up the tower, with our big snowflake on top."

"No problem," said Reddy.

Katie and Dylan watched as Reddy's crew flew around the tower and hung lights.

"Put some in the trees, too," said Papa.

"No problem," said Reddy, and his crew started on it.

"And inside the house, give me one switch to turn them all on and off."

"No problem," said Reddy.

"Can we help turn them on every night, Papa?" asked Katie.

"Of course," said Papa. "We'll do it together."

AVIAN
SERVICES
"Flying Your Way"

CHRISTMAS TREES

On Saturday morning, Papa drove with Katie and Dylan to the Christmas tree farm. It was snowy, and twinkling with lights. There were trees of all sizes.

"Big tree!" squeaked Dylan. He tried to see the top and almost fell over backwards.

"That's for an outdoor Christmas tree, like in the town square," Papa told him.

"Look at this pretty little one!" said Katie.

"That's for a table top in a smaller home," said Papa, rubbing his paws together. "We need a tree just the right size for our living room."

They found the perfect one. The farmer helped carry it to their car. "Merry Christmas!" he called after them.

"See train now?" asked Dylan.

That afternoon, Cousin Matilda came and took Katie shopping. They could hardly believe how dressed up Mouse Town was, and how it sparkled. “It’s all so beautiful!” Katie squeaked.

They stopped in front of the Mouse Town Gift Shop. Katie pointed to a shiny red train in the window. “Dylan would love that.”

“Maybe Santa Mouse will bring him one,” said Matilda. “What do *you* want to give him?”

“A book with train pictures,” said Katie.

“What about for your Mama?”

Katie looked at the shop window again. “She’d love those silk flowers.”

“Great idea,” said Matilda. “And for Papa?”

“Mittens,” said Katie. “His paws get cold when he’s outside.”

“And what about you, Katie? What do you want from Santa Mouse?”

“I can’t decide.”

Matilda looked puzzled. “So, you know what everyone else would like, but not yourself? Maybe a pretty dress?”

“I don’t know,” said Katie. “Maybe.”

But she couldn’t help hoping for something else from Santa Mouse—something magical. She just didn’t know what!

MOUSE TOWN GIFTS

'Twas the night before Christmas

Back at home, Katie wrapped her gifts for the family and put them under the tree. The living room was as beautiful as Mouse Town, decorated with shiny red and green. And every evening, when Katie and Dylan helped Papa turn on the lights, the house glittered and sparkled on the outside, too.

Finally, it was Christmas Eve. At bedtime, Mama pulled up a chair and read a story to Katie. But she was still wide-awake at the end.

"Try to sleep, Katie," Mama said. "Santa Mouse won't come any faster if you're awake."

"Mama, what did you do at Christmastime when you were little?"

"My brothers and I liked to tumble in the snow, just like you and your friends. Or we'd go skating, or look at snowflakes with a magnifying glass. And on Christmas Eve, we tried to stay awake to see Santa Mouse—but we never could."

"Mama, I could never decide what I want. What if Santa Mouse brings me something I don't like?"

"Don't worry, Katie. Santa Mouse is a pretty good guesser. Now, close your eyes and imagine snow falling very, very gently. Watch the snowflakes, and morning will come before you know it."

With her eyes shut, Katie watched the snowflakes, and soon she was fast asleep.

Late that night, while Katie slept, Santa Mouse and his mouse elves came to the house.

Santa Mouse listened to make sure no one was awake, then nodded to the elves. They started filling Katie's and Dylan's stockings and setting presents under the tree. Quickly and quietly they worked—all except Alvar Elf, who spotted the lovely plate of cookies Mama had baked for them.

"Christmas cookies!" squeaked Alvar, who was helping Santa Mouse for the very first time.

"Ssssshhh!" said Santa Mouse. "Alvar, don't you remember the rule?"

Alvar said sheepishly, *"Presents first, cookies last."*

"That's right," said Santa Mouse. "We'll all have cookies when we're done."

But Alvar loved cookies so much! While everyone was busy, he backed toward the goodies. Keeping an eye on Santa Mouse and the others, he grabbed a cookie and snuck a nibble.

"This is a great house," he thought. "Wonder what's up in that tower we saw."

He opened a door and found stairs. "I bet those lead right up to that tower," he thought. He glanced back, but the others were all busy with presents.

"I'll just be a minute," he thought. "No one will ever miss me."

Katie woke up, startled. She was sure she'd heard her door open. She switched on her lamp and saw a mouse elf eating a cookie.

"Who are you?" she asked. "And what are you doing here?"

"I'm Alvar. Everyone's busy downstairs, so I came up to check out the tower." He shoved the last of the cookie into his mouth.

"*Everyone's* busy?" said Katie, her eyes wide. "Does that mean Santa Mouse and his elves?"

"Funny mouse," said a voice behind Alvar, and Dylan toddled into the room.

Alvar looked from Dylan to Katie and back. "I don't think I should be here," he said. "I better go."

"Wait!" said Katie. "Is Santa Mouse really here?" She threw back the covers and stepped into her slippers, ready to rush downstairs.

"Stop!" said Alvar. "You can't go down there! I'd be in *so* much trouble!"

Katie really wanted to see Santa Mouse, but she didn't want to get Alvar in trouble. "Then please tell us all about the North Pole!"

"I really should get back," said Alvar nervously.

"Wait!" said Katie. "What's it like up there? Where do you all live?"

Alvar's eyes lit up. "Oh, you should see it! We live with Santa Mouse in a beautiful castle, with high towers and grand balconies. And outside is a big reindeer barn, and a skating pool, and a magical forest, and a train that runs around all of it."

"Train!" squeaked Dylan, and clapped his paws.

"And Santa Mouse's workshop?" Katie asked.

"That too!" said Alvar. "It's where we make all the toys!"

"Would they let us come inside, if we went there?"

"Maybe not," said Alvar. "There are safety rules, you know, and secrets we need to keep."

Katie couldn't help but look disappointed.

"But you could go in the magical forest," Alvar added quickly. "That's where we have the Christmas Door."

"What's the Christmas Door?" Katie asked with new interest.

Alvar's eyes shone even brighter. "When the Christmas Door opens, it shows you what you want and need the most."

"That sounds wonderful!" said Katie. "I can never decide that for myself." She sighed. "But I guess I could never go there."

Alvar thought a moment. "You don't really need to. I could show it to both of you, right here."

"Really?" said Katie, all excited.

"Just close your eyes and look for a red and green door at the end of a path. I'll help you."

Katie and Dylan closed their eyes. Snow swirled all around them, thick and soft. As it settled, they found themselves on a misty forest path with Alvar.

The mist grew thinner, and out of it, a door slowly appeared before them—red and green with gold trimmings, brighter than their Christmas tree. A gold key hung from the doorknob.

“What do we do now?” said Katie.

“Just touch the key, and the door will open,” said Alvar. “Who’s first?”

“Me!” squeaked Dylan.

Katie smiled and helped Dylan walk along the snowy path. As he touched the key, the door vanished. A shriek filled the air, and a light like the sun rushed toward them.

Katie squealed in fright, jumping back and pulling Dylan with her. But Dylan only laughed and waved his paws. “Train! Train!” he squeaked.

That’s what it was, Katie saw. And it was headed straight for them!

“Don’t be afraid,” Alvar yelled over the train’s roar. “It can’t hurt us. It’s only a picture in his mind.”

Just as the train reached them, the door clanged shut. Katie’s heart hammered, as Dylan squealed in delight.

“Your turn now,” Alvar told Katie.

“I’m not sure . . .” she began.

“Don’t worry,” he said. “Yours won’t be so scary.”

She touched the key softly and got ready to jump away. But this time, the door faded slowly, and there was nothing glaring or blaring.

Katie heard voices and peered in. What she saw was herself! There she was in the living room on Christmas morning, with Mama and Papa and Dylan.

There were lights and laughter. Then Katie and Dylan climbed onto the laps of Mama and Papa, who hugged them both together.

The door faded back into place. The snow swirled around them again, and Katie opened her eyes. She was back in her own room with Dylan and Alvar.

“I still didn’t see what I want,” she said sadly. “It only showed our family tomorrow morning.”

“But isn’t . . .” began Alvar. Suddenly, his eyes grew wide and his face grew pale. “Uh-oh. Do I hear jingle bells?”

They raced to the balcony outside Katie's room. In the moonlight, they saw Santa Mouse and the elves in their sleigh, and the reindeer pulling it across the snow.

"Come back! Come back!" they shouted.

But Santa Mouse and the elves couldn't hear them over the sleigh bells, and the sleigh lifted off without Alvar.

"Oh my snowy whiskers!" cried the elf. "How will I ever get back to the North Pole?"

"The Christmas lights!" Katie squeaked. "Quick!"

With Alvar bringing Dylan behind, Katie scrambled through her room and out to the switch in the hall. She stretched up and flipped it on, then off, then on, again and again.

High in the sky, Santa Mouse saw the Christmas lights blink. "Looks like a signal!" he said. "Could that be for us?"

The elves looked around. "Where's Alvar?" said one, and another answered, "We must have left him behind!"

"Rookies and cookies!" muttered Santa Mouse as he turned the sleigh around.

The lights were staying on now, and Santa Mouse could see three mice on the balcony, jumping and waving and squeaking. He guided the sleigh to float beside the railing.

"Alvar!" scolded Santa Mouse. "Tell me the rule you broke this time!"

"*Work, don't wander,*" squeaked the shamefaced elf as he scrambled into the sleigh.

Santa Mouse shook his head, but he was smiling kindly, and so were the other elves as they teased their friend. So, Katie knew Alvar wasn't in *too* much trouble.

"Wait, Santa Mouse," said Katie. "I could never decide what I want this year. And when Alvar brought us to the Christmas Door, it wouldn't show me."

"No?" said Santa Mouse with a chuckle. "Well, don't worry, Katie. I have a feeling you'll get exactly what you want most."

"Me, too," yelled Dylan. "Train!"

"Yes, you too, Dylan," said Santa Mouse with a smile.

He twitched the reins, and the sleigh slipped away as quick as an eyeblink. Katie watched it as long as she could, but in moments, it had vanished among the twinkling stars.

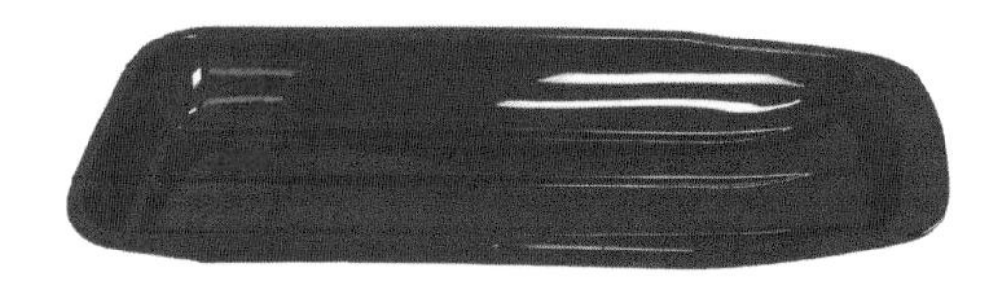

When Katie woke the next morning, bright sunshine glittered through frost on the window. As she got out of bed, Mama looked in.

"Santa Mouse came last night!" said Mama. "Come down and see!"

Katie found her slippers and robe, quickly washed and dried her furry face, and went downstairs to the living room. Dylan was playing with a train that looked just like the one in the gift shop window.

"Train!" he squeaked, waving at her.

Then she saw what was beside the tree. "A sled!" she squeaked happily. Why hadn't she thought to ask for that? She imagined hours and hours of sledding with her friends.

But still, was that what she wanted most, or what Santa Mouse had said she'd get? It wasn't what the Christmas Door had shown her.

Then Katie turned around and saw it—the scene from the Christmas Door. Mama and Papa and Dylan. The lights and the laughter and the love.

And suddenly she knew what she wanted and needed most. It wasn't a present at all! It was Christmas at home with her family!

Katie rushed to the sofa and jumped onto Papa's lap.

"Our wonderful daughter," said Mama, as she and Papa wrapped her in a big mouse hug.

"Me, too!" squealed Dylan, climbing up to join in.

"We love you both so much," said Papa.

And Katie couldn't think of any gift more magical than that!

Consulting and editing by Aaron Shepard
Ages 4–9

Version 1.0

## About Anne and Mouse Town

In 2016, Anne L. Watson fell in love with felted mice by Bulgarian artist Diyana Stankova. Anne happened to be working on a housekeeping almanac, so she started photographing the mice, posing them in scenes with miniatures in dollhouses, to illustrate the book. Soon she was writing little stories about the mouse family, while learning to use Photoshop to manipulate their poses and composite their props and settings in a creative blend of toys, other photos, and purchased and free art.

As Anne added more mice and other felted animals from Diyana and other artists, Mouse Town began to take shape. As might be expected, these adorable but pushy critters eventually demanded their own books, and Anne obliged with the Katie Mouse series.

Besides her children's books, Anne writes literary novels and how-to books for grown-ups, on such subjects as housekeeping, soapmaking, and baking with cookie molds. She lives in Bellingham, Washington, with her husband and fellow author, Aaron Shepard, and a growing family of critters. Visit her at **www.annelwatson.com**.

## Credits

Felted mice and guinea pig by Diyana Stankova • Chipmunk by Shells Mystic Felts • Hedgehog by Dalia and Nerijus Kisieliai • Hamster by HandmadeByNovember • Squirrel by ClaudiaMarieFelt • Birds by St. Placid Priory • Fireplace by Gooseberry Creek • Mouse house by CosediunaltroMondo • Christmas tree by Studebaker Miniatures • Santa's castle by Bea Fallon • Lamppost by Kate Smith Photography • Books in bookcase by Snaphaven • Flower arrangement by Vintage Retro Antique • Dresses by Digital Paper Craft • Mirror frame by Skandia Design Studio • Dishes by Daria Konik • Door by Blossoms Digi Shop • Key by Star Designs • Fawn by Kate Smith Photography • Star on tower by Pomp Owl • Mittens by Ham Ham Art • Amigurumi mouse by CROriginals • Carousel by LasMinisdeMaini • Toy blocks by SweetkarmaStore • Embroidered pillows by ViolasNeedfulThings • Patchwork quilts by AlphabetStore • Christmas cookies by CrystalGraphic

*Also with Katie Mouse . . .*

CPSIA information can be obtained at www.ICGtesting.com
Printed in the USA
BVIW12n1110260118
506384BV00014B/210

Cover design and formatting Tim Noble

First published 2021

It's a rather special day at Mixed Up Zoo.

Everyone's excited and I hope you are too!

The carnival's in town! Now let's find a seat,

I think we are in for a mixed up treat!

The carnival's here- what a great show!

What animal's first? I think I might know...

First up on stage and look at him juggle.

It's an underwater whalerus, blowing **big bubbles!**

*Up! Up! Up!* Round they go! We don't want him to stop!

But the trouble with bubbles is bubbles- they **pop!**

Pop!

The carnival's here!

What a great show!

What animal's next?

I think I might know...

**Blasting** his music and speaking in rhyme,

It's a *small,* *spikey* creature, a pigupine.

He's rapping and singing and speaking so *fast,*

Thank goodness **that** performance is over at last!

The carnival's here!

What a great show!

What animal's next?

I think I might know...

Ah, now this is more like it, the **best** one yet.

It's orangucan with his **black** clarinet.

The music is perfect, it's so *swish* and so **sleek**

But how does he manage those notes from a beak?

The carnival's here!

What a great show!

What animal's next?

I think I might know...

Wobbling and wibbling, here comes the next act.
Balancing on ropes like an acrobat!
Be careful zeebear, you look far too heavy!
And that line you are on doesn't look very steady!

The carnival's here!

What a great show!

What animal's next?

I think I might know...

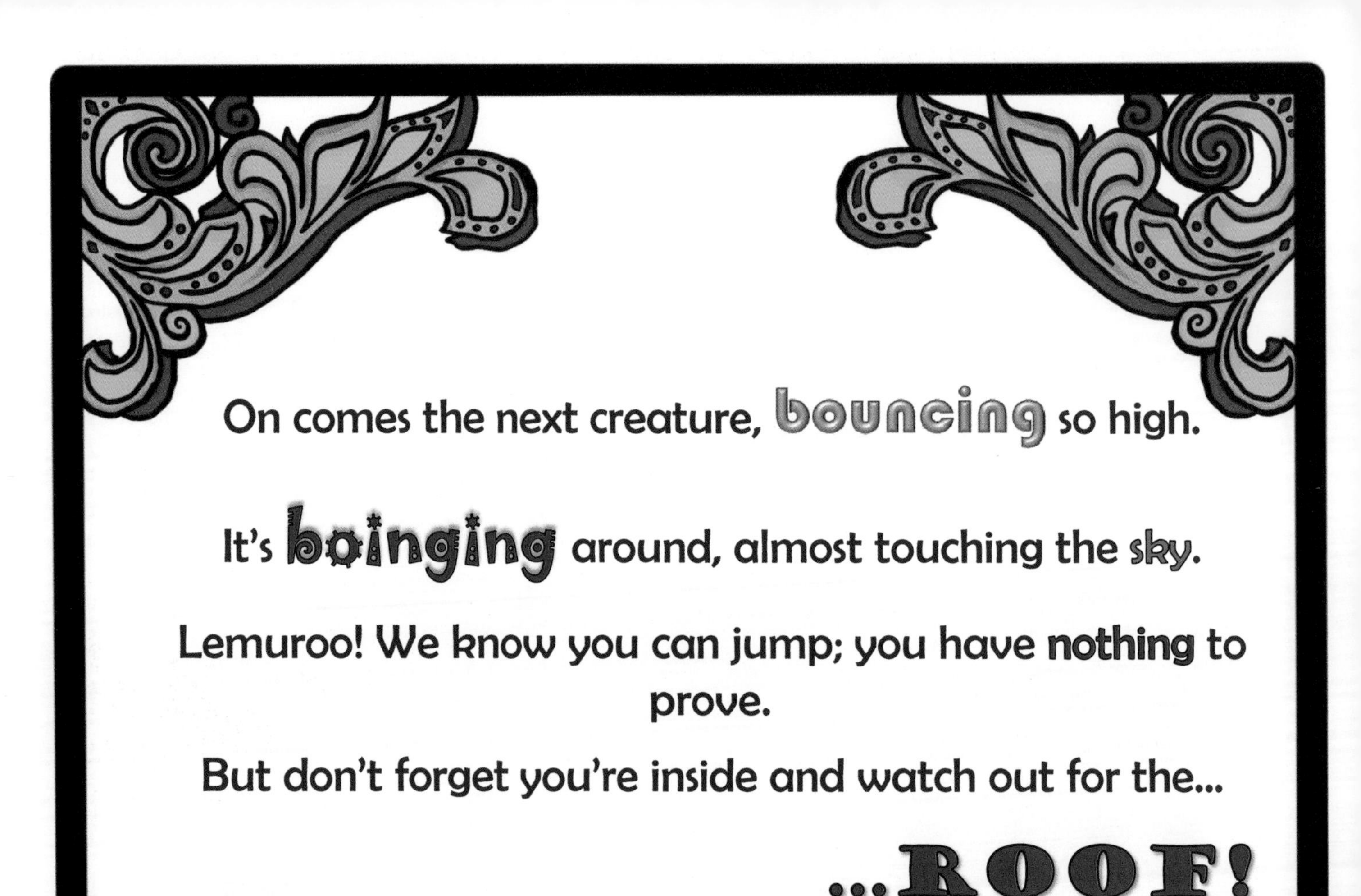

On comes the next creature, bouncing so high.

It's boinging around, almost touching the sky.

Lemuroo! We know you can jump; you have **nothing** to prove.

But don't forget you're inside and watch out for the...

...ROOF!

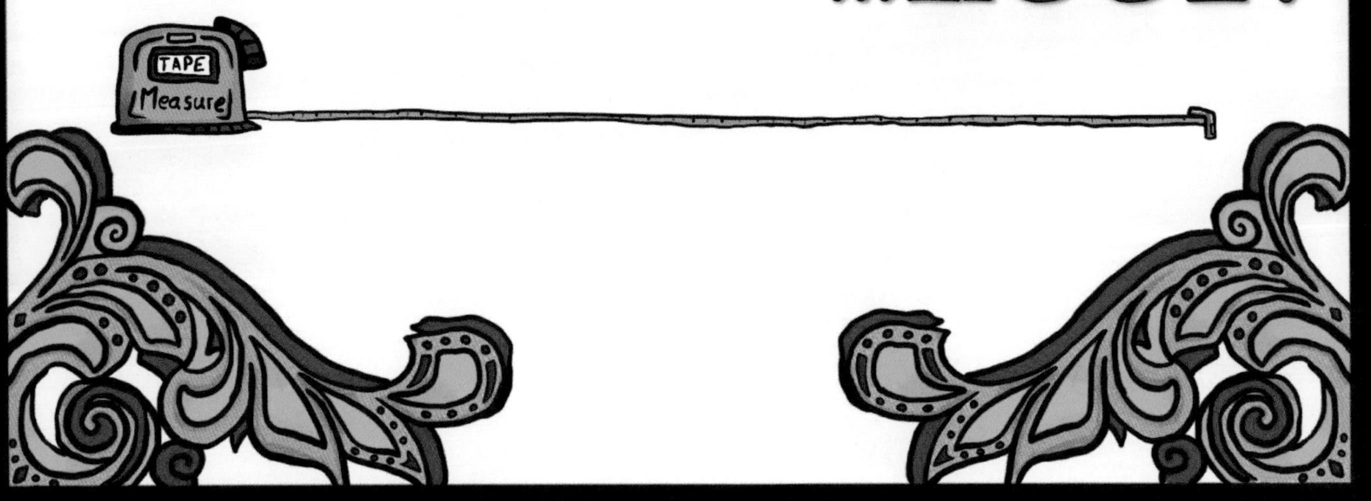

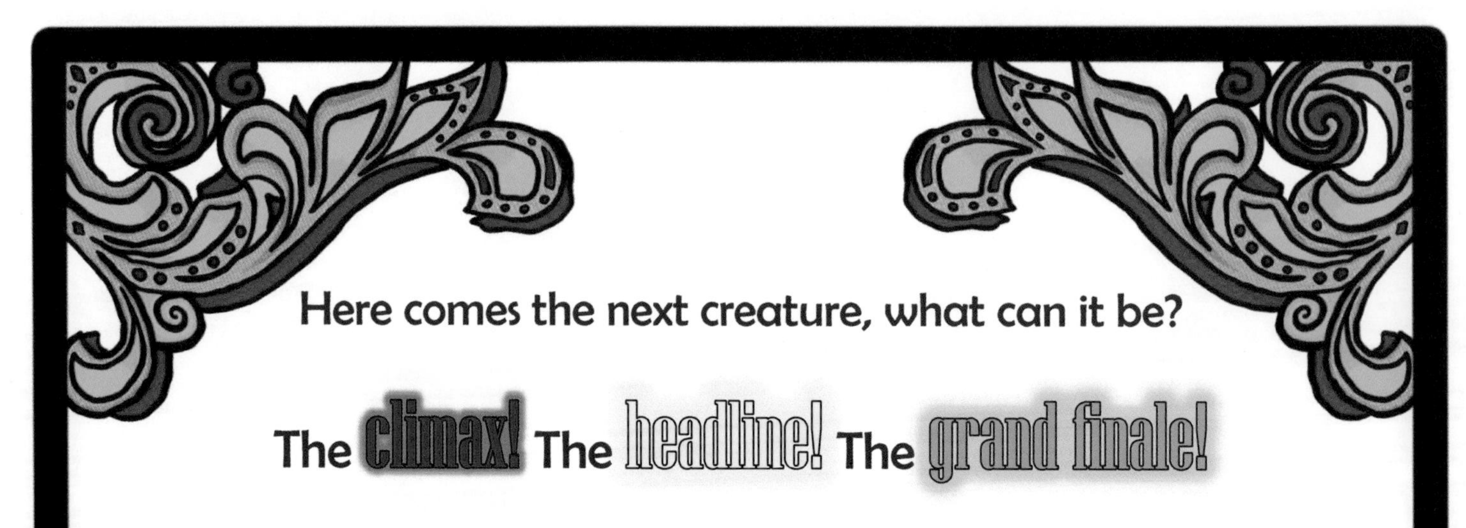

Here comes the next creature, what can it be?

The climax! The headline! The grand finale!

We've had so many tricks and so much fun,

The applause ripples round, the last act's begun...

The whole tent falls silent, no one dares says a word;

Not even the sound of dropped pins can be heard.

Then onto the stage steps a creature quite strange-

A mixed up animal, but what is its name?

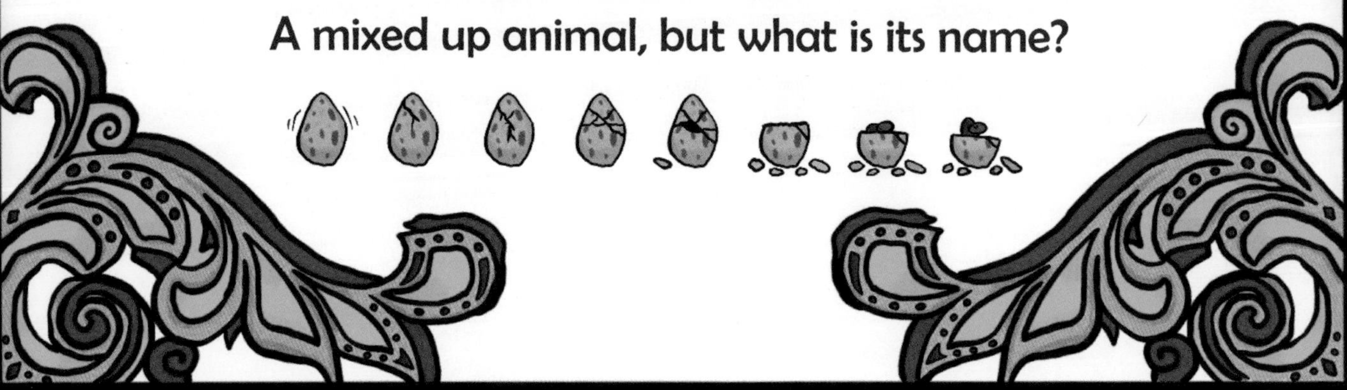

"**Wait a minute,**" purrs the slynx,

"**I've not sssSSeen you before!**

**You're not mixed up, you're real, I'm sure**"

"A REAL animal?" a whisper goes through the crowd,

"What's he doing on stage, that can't be allowed?"

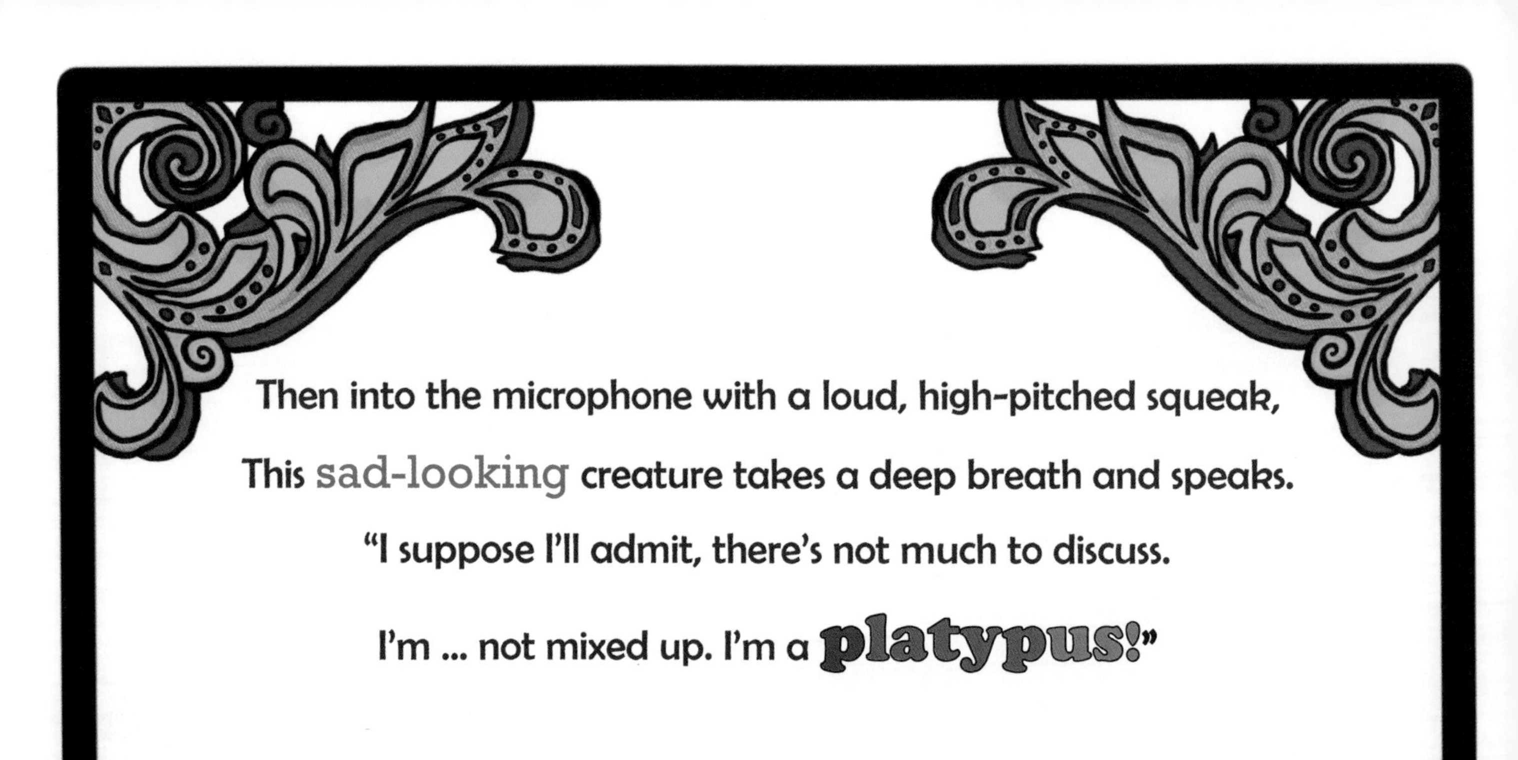

Then into the microphone with a loud, high-pitched squeak,

This sad-looking creature takes a deep breath and speaks.

"I suppose I'll admit, there's not much to discuss.

I'm ... not mixed up. I'm a platypus!"

"You see, I heard all the music, the fun and the laughter.

So, I slipped in the tent and past the ringmaster.

I thought I could join in at this carnival show

But I can see I'm not wanted so I'll guess I'll just go..."

"**Wait!**" said the owlephant, "I have something to say,

You don't have to leave here! We'd *love* you to stay!

As, although you are real, you are still one of us.

We turn **NO ONE** away, including you, platypus."

"For no matter how different or ODD you may feel

Or how far from home or like a square wheel,

There's a place here for everyone, a place here for you.

We're all mixed up creatures at Mixed Up Zoo."

Printed in Great Britain
by Amazon